In memory of our first editor, Elke Lacey,
and for her son, Fred.

First published in 1993 by Methuen Children's Books

First published in 2003 by Macmillan Children's Books
A division of Macmillan Publishers Limited
20 New Wharf Road, London N1 9RR
Basingstoke and Oxford
Associated companies throughout the world
This edition produced 2004 for The Book People Ltd,
Hall Wood Avenue, Haydock, St Helens WA11 9UL

ISBN 1 405 00476 2

5 7 9 8 6 4

A CIP catalogue record for this book is available from the British Library.

Printed in China

A Squash and a Squeeze

Story by
Julia Donaldson

Illustrated by
Axel Scheffler

TED SMART

A little old lady lived all by herself
With a table and chairs and a jug on the shelf.

A wise old man heard her grumble and grouse,
"There's not enough room in my house.
Wise old man, won't you help me, please?
My house is a squash and a squeeze."

"Take in your hen," said the wise old man.

"Take in my hen? What a curious plan."

Well, the hen laid an egg on the fireside rug,

And flapped round the room knocking over the jug.

The little old lady cried, "What shall I do?
It was poky for one and it's tiny for two.
My nose has a tickle and there's no room to sneeze.
My house is a squash and a squeeze."

And she said, "Wise old man,
    won't you help me, please?
My house is a squash and a squeeze."

"Take in your goat," said the wise old man.

"Take in my goat? What a curious plan."

Well, the goat chewed the curtains and trod on the egg,

then sat down to nibble the table leg.

The little old lady cried, "Glory be!
It was tiny for two and it's titchy for three.
The hen pecks the goat and the goat's got fleas.
My house is a squash and a squeeze."

And she said, "Wise old man,
    won't you help me, please?
My house is a squash and a squeeze."

"Take in your pig," said the wise old man.

"Take in my pig? What a curious plan."

So she took in her pig who kept chasing the hen,

And raiding the larder again and again.

The little old lady cried, "Stop, I implore!
It was titchy for three and it's teeny for four.
Even the pig in the larder agrees,
My house is a squash and a squeeze."

And she said, "Wise old man,
    won't you help me, please?
My house is a squash and a squeeze."

"Take in your cow," said the wise old man.

"Take in my cow? What a curious plan."

Well, the cow took one look and charged straight at the pig,
Then jumped on the table and tapped out a jig.

The little old lady cried, "Heavens alive!
It was teeny for four and it's weeny for five.
I'm tearing my hair out, I'm down on my knees.
My house is a squash and a squeeze."

And she said, "Wise old man,
    won't you help me, please?
My house is a squash and a squeeze."

"Take them all out," said the wise old man.
"But then I'll be back where I first began."

So she opened the window and out flew the hen.
"That's better – at last I can sneeze again."

She shooed out the goat and she shoved out the pig.
"My house is beginning to feel pretty big."

She huffed and she puffed and she pushed out the cow.
"Just look at my house, it's enormous now.

"Thank you, old man, for the work you have done.
It was weeny for five, it's gigantic for one.
There's no need to grumble and there's no need to grouse.
There's plenty of room in my house."

And now she's full of frolics and fiddle-de-dees.
It isn't a squash and it isn't a squeeze.

Yes, she's full of frolics and fiddle-de-dees.
It isn't a squash or a squeeze.

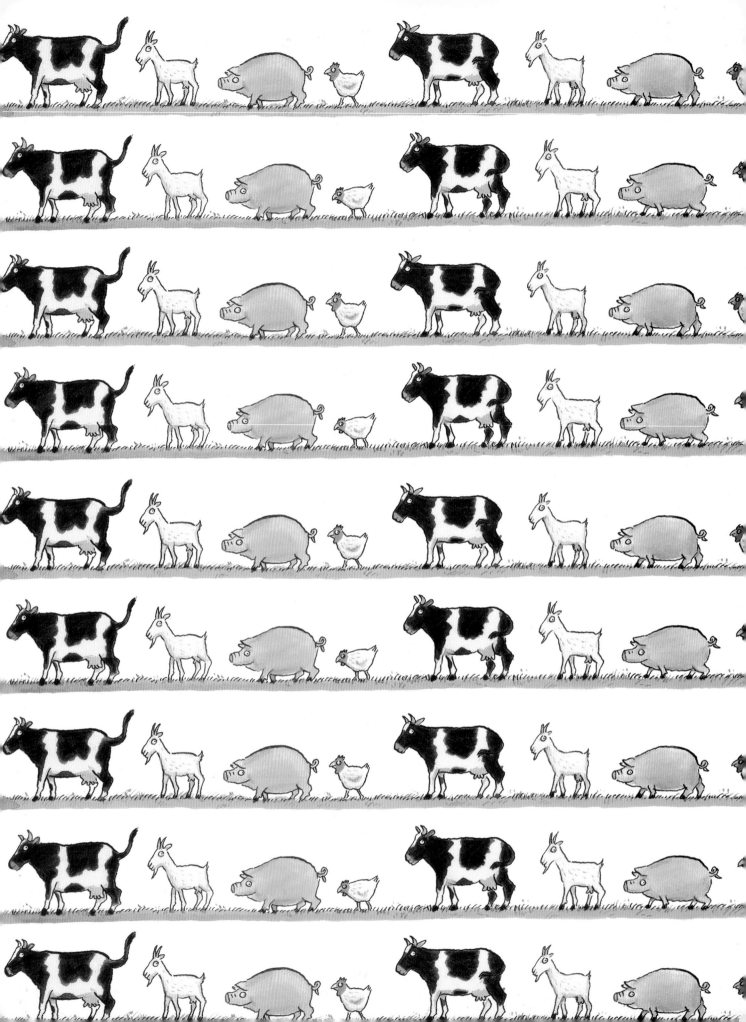

TALES for a PRINCE

Foreword

In a nationwide competition, sponsored by C&A, schoolchildren were invited to write a bedtime story for Prince Henry of Wales. The fifteen stories in this collection are written by the winners of the competition, chosen from a huge entry, and each story is professionally illustrated.

The competition, and publication of this book, are designed to raise funds for UNICEF, the United Nations Children's Fund.

Every year in the developing world nearly four million children under five die from six preventable child killing diseases: whooping cough, diphtheria, tuberculosis, polio, measles and tetanus. Many die because they do not have access to health centres, or vaccine, or trained medical workers.

UNICEF has set a goal of ending this tragic waste of young lives through a campaign for universal childhood immunisation by 1990. To achieve this goal, UNICEF will use the funds raised to support this programme.

A copy of TALES FOR A PRINCE has been accepted by Her Royal Highness the Princess of Wales for Prince Henry.

TALES FOR A PRINCE COMPETITION

sponsored by

in aid of

TALES for a PRINCE

HODDER AND STOUGHTON
LONDON SYDNEY AUCKLAND TORONTO

The publishers would like to acknowledge the assistance of the following companies in the manufacture of this book: Cambus Litho, East Kilbride; Hunter and Foulis Ltd, Edinburgh; Townsend Hook Ltd, Snodland, Kent; Ecran Offset Ltd, Croydon, Surrey; Duraglaze Ltd, Mitcham, Surrey; Dot Gradations Ltd, South Woodham Ferrers, Essex; Rowland Phototypesetting (London) Ltd.

British Library Cataloguing in Publication Data

Tales for a prince.
 1. Children's short stories in English.
 1945– —Anthologies
 823′.01′089282[J]

 ISBN 0-340-42658-6

Text copyright © UNICEF-UK 1988
Illustrations copyright © UNICEF-UK 1988

First published 1988

Published by Hodder and Stoughton Children's Books,
a division of Hodder and Stoughton Ltd,
Mill Road, Dunton Green, Sevenoaks, Kent TN13 2YJ

Book design: Trevor Spooner

Printed and bound in Great Britain

Contents

Have You seen My Boot? *by Iain Hollands, age 11*   10

The Matchbox Magnificent *by Dee Enright, age 12*   12

The Giraffe with a Knot in Its Neck *by Jonathan Gough, age 13*   14

The Kangaroo who could not Bounce *by Oliver Kubicki, age 10*   17

Magic Paper *by William Woods, age 13*   18

Nigel the Naughty Spider *by Rachel West, age 15*   20

Time Traviler *by Gordon Semple, age 7*   22

The Lonely Dragon *by Joanne Haughton, age 13*   24

Henry's Orange Machine *by Helen Pates, age 14*   27

Safer to be Albert *by Mark van Leuwen, age 11*   30

Hippo's Fruit Bowl *by Sophie Annesley, age 10*   32

The Mouse with Big Ears *by Rebecca Bryan, age 8*   34

King Midas and his Touch of Jelly *by Michelle Normand, age 11*   36

A Tall Story *by Leigh Johnston, age 12*   39

Santa gets Stuck *by Rebecca Niblock and Emma Boyns, both age 10*   42

Illustrated by Larry Wilkes

Have You seen My Boot?

by Iain Hollands

One day, early in the morning, Chris the Centipede was putting on his boots. This took lots of time because he had to put a hundred boots on a hundred legs.

'95, 96, 97, 98...' Chris counted as he put them on, '...99, hey, where has my last boot gone?' Chris wondered because he couldn't see it.

'I wonder if I'm sitting on it,' he said. 'No.'

'I wonder if I'm standing on it,' he thought. 'No.'

'I wonder if it's under the bed,' he asked. 'No.'

'I wonder if it's in the cupboard,' he wondered. 'No.'

He decided to go out and ask if any of his friends in the garden had seen his boot. First he saw Millie the Millipede.

'Hello, have you seen my boot?' Chris asked.

'No, but Anthea the Ant might have,' Millie told him. So Chris went on until he met Anthea the Ant.

'Hello, you have seen my boot?' Chris asked.

'No, but Wally the Wasp might have,' Anthea replied. Soon Chris met Wally.

'Have you seen my boot?' Chris asked.

'No,' Wally replied.

Now Chris really did not know where his boot was. Then he saw Darren the Dragonfly Dustman. *Now* he remembered what he had done with his boot. It had had a hole in it and he had put it in the bin. He had to go to Sam Snail's Shoe Shop to get a new one.

What a silly centipede!

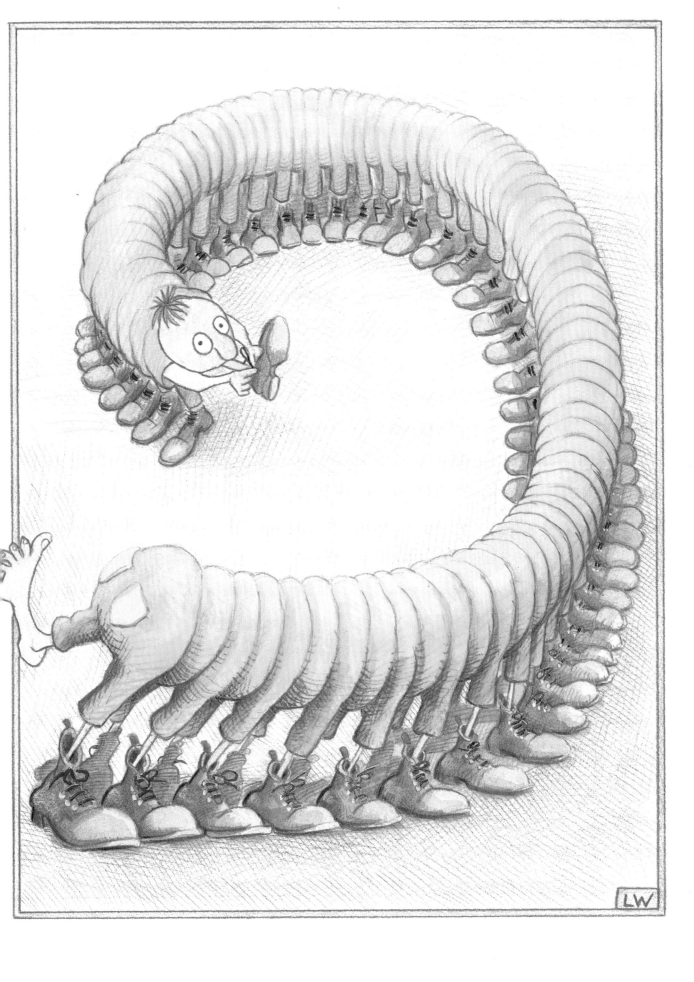

Illustrated by Bob Wilson

The Matchbox Magnificent

by Dee Enright

Harold was a little boy who, when he was small, decided to start collecting matchboxes. From then on, whenever anyone was about to throw away a matchbox, he would cry, 'Stop. Wait. May I have that matchbox please?' And he would have yet another to add to his collection. In fact, he had so many that once Harold's mother said to him, 'You have so many of these silly matchboxes that you could get lost in them.' But Harold would never throw any away, not even one.

Of course, he always made sure that they were empty because he was a sensible little boy, and Mum had always said that matches could be very, very dangerous indeed.

One day while he was reading a book Harold had an idea, a fantastic idea. Surely, if he had enough matchboxes to get lost in, he had enough to make what he wanted more than anything – a rocket ship! Yes, it must be possible.

So, leaping from his chair, Harold took a pot of glue from his drawer, collected together all of his matchboxes and, glueing faster than he had ever glued before, Harold stuck matchbox to matchbox and that matchbox to yet another, and slowly but surely the rocket ship started to take shape.

When it came to fixing together the higher parts of Harold's creation, he needed to stand on a chair to reach. But when every box had been used up and it had come to the last finishing touches, he took his paintbox and painted on the side in big red letters:

THE MATCHBOX MAGNIFICENT

He stood back to admire the fabulous model that he had made. It really was magnificent. Harold clambered inside. It began to tremble, a rumbling started from deep inside. It gave a little jump and then it began to rise upwards. Through Harold's bedroom ceiling, up through the roof and out into the evening air.

The rocket ship kept on climbing and at one point Harold actually reached out of the window and caught a shooting star. He then took a sip of the Milky Way and waved to a couple of little blue Martians in a passing flying saucer. Harold was very pleased when they waved back.

It soon began to get very cold and dark and Harold yawned. Gosh, he hadn't noticed how very tired he was. So he turned the rocket ship about and headed back towards home.

The next day was Mum's birthday and Harold made his way past the enormous rocket ship standing in the middle of his bedroom floor, down the stairs and to the breakfast table where his mother was opening her presents.

'Here is your present from me, Mum,' said Harold handing her a small glittering star.

'Oh Harold, it's lovely!' she said. 'Where did you get it?'

'You'd never believe me if I told you,' Harold said smiling happily. 'Oh, and Dad, sorry about the hole in the roof!'

Illustrated by Martin Ursell

The Giraffe with a Knot in Its Neck

by Jonathan Gough

One day Giraffe woke up with a strange feeling. A strange, peculiar feeling. Giraffe did not realise that he had a knot in his neck.

'I wonder why I feel strange,' Giraffe thought to himself. 'I know. I'm hungry. That's what's wrong.'

So Giraffe went to the banana tree at the edge of the jungle. He chose the ripest banana and bit it off the tree, swallowing it whole. The banana got stuck half way down his throat. Wondering what was wrong, Giraffe looked down at his long, long neck.

'Oh no!' Giraffe exclaimed. 'What can I do?'

He saw the knot in his neck. Giraffe decided to go for a walk to cheer himself up.

On his way he passed Monkey's tree where Monkey was swinging happily. A tear ran down Giraffe's cheek.

'What's up?' Monkey shouted from the treetops.

'I've got this great big knot in my neck. Could you help me?' Giraffe answered.

'I could try to pull it free,' Monkey said.

So Monkey climbed down from his tree and grabbed Giraffe's neck and said, 'Get ready Giraffe. One, two, three ... pull!'

Monkey pulled and pulled, but he just could not get the knot from Giraffe's neck.

'I'm sorry, Giraffe. Go and ask Elephant. He's much stronger than me.'

So Giraffe went to find Elephant. He found him by the lake. Seeing Giraffe's face, Elephant asked, 'What's wrong Giraffe?'

'I've got this great big knot in my neck. Could you help me?'

'I could try to shrink it out using some water from the lake,' Elephant said.

He took one big slurp with his trunk and aimed it at Giraffe's neck. SPLASH! The water soaked Giraffe's neck.

It didn't work. The knot was not gone and Giraffe started to cry.

'Don't cry,' Elephant said.

But Giraffe cried and cried, saying, 'What can I do? What can I do?'

Elephant suddenly had an idea.

'Go and see wise old Snail. He'll tell you what to do.'

Giraffe, thinking there was nothing else to do, set off to find Snail. He was feeling hungry because he couldn't swallow any food because of the knot in

his neck. While thinking of food, he bumped into Snail.

'Hello Snail. I've got a problem,' Giraffe told him.

'What sort of problem?' Snail asked.

'I've got this great big knot in my neck. Could you help me?'

Snail thought a bit.

'Mmmm. Come to my hole in the big tree.' Giraffe followed him.

Once inside, Giraffe looked around Snail's house. Bookcases, lined with books, littered the place, Snail opened a large red book which was on one of the bookcases. It was called *Problems*.

'Now, let's see,' Snail muttered to himself. 'Shrinking heads, disappearing spots, lost teeth. Ah, here it is: A Knot in the Neck. Oh dear, it's been scribbled out. I'm sorry, Giraffe. I don't know what to do.'

Giraffe went home feeling very sad. It started to get dark and he fell asleep.

In the morning Giraffe woke up and looked at his neck.

'Yippeee!' he shouted.

The knot had disappeared.

While Giraffe was shouting for joy, Monkey, Elephant, Snail and all the other jungle animals ran up to Giraffe looking very sad.

'What's up?' asked Giraffe:

The animals answered together.

'I've got this great big knot in my neck. Could you help me?'

Giraffe gave out a loud groan.

'Oh no. Not again!' he said.

Illustrated by Babette Cole

The Kangaroo who could not Bounce

by Oliver Kubicki

Deep in the heart of the Australian bush there lived a family of kangaroos.

Mother was sitting quietly under a eucalyptus tree surrounded by her four baby roos. Baby Kanga was too young to be out of his mother's pouch, so he peeped out.

Mother gave all the roos bouncing lessons and running lessons. The roos learned very quickly but Mother thought Baby Kanga was still too young.

Once when Mother left him he made friends with Wally Wallaby. A few years later all his brothers and sisters were able to run and bounce miles in a few seconds.

Poor Baby Kanga tried to copy his brothers and sisters, but much as he tried he just could not do it. This made him very unhappy.

Wally Wallaby was hunting in the bush when he discovered an old wreck of a car. Sticking out of the back he found some springs. He thought of an idea to help Baby Kanga. He picked up the springs and chased back to unhappy Baby Kanga. He showed Baby Kanga how to fix the springs to his feet, and told him to copy him.

Wally jumped up and down and Kanga copied. To Kanga's amazement, he discovered he could bounce. He was so happy.

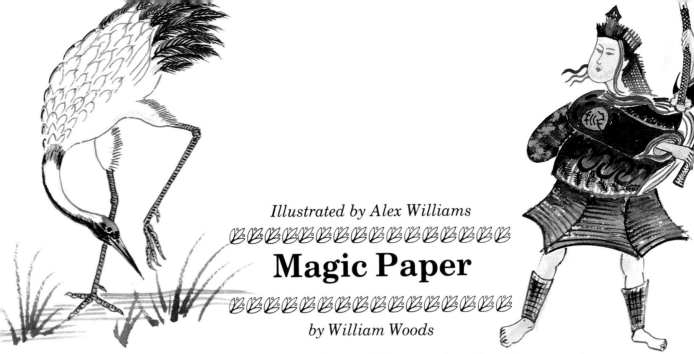

Illustrated by Alex Williams

Magic Paper

by William Woods

A long time ago, in a far off land we call Japan, there lived a young boy called Itoh. He lived near a small fishing village by the sea with his old grandfather.

The people were very poor, even poorer than peasants in other villages, because the lord who owned the nearby lands was extremely greedy and taxed the people terribly. Sometimes people couldn't even get enough money to feed their families for a day or two. They were all very angry, but dared not complain for fear of the lord's mighty samurai soldiers.

Itoh's grandfather was a kindly man and the two got on well together. He was a hermit and never saw many people where he lived. So, to pass the time, he used to practise origami, the ancient art of paper folding. He could make animals at the flick of a wrist, and birds were easy. Itoh soon picked up the skills, and his grandfather gave him ten sheets of paper.

'They are magical,' he explained. 'When you have finished folding a shape, blow on it and it will become real.'

Itoh soon boosted his fortune and the village's by making models of animals and buildings and trees, and anything you could possibly think of. People came from miles around to buy his models because the magic of the paper made sure all his shapes were perfect. He never blew on his creations for fear he would be imprisoned for sorcery.

But one day, when he was shaping a crane, a gust of wind blew past the paper, and a real bird leapt forward and flew away. Itoh's secret was out.

The story spread through the land faster than the crane had sprung, and soon Itoh was ordered to appear before the evil lord, Saito.

Saito was a very greedy and cruel man who had no love for honour and a heart of stone. He wanted to rule the whole of Japan, so when he discovered Itoh's magic he was very excited.

18

'What can you make with that paper?' he asked Itoh eagerly.

'Anything practically. But I don't think…' Itoh was interrupted.

'Can you make me an army?' Saito enquired.

'Well I've only got one sheet left, so…'

'What can you make then?' He seemed annoyed.

'I can make birds and flowers and animals and oh, so many things.' Itoh became nervous and fumbled.

Saito sat and thought and suddenly an idea struck him. 'Can you make big things – VERY BIG THINGS?'

'Um, well, I can make houses if you want. But, if you please, I don't see…' The boy began to mumble.

The fat lord laughed. 'Could you make me a dragon? A great big golden dragon?'

'Um, well, I suppose so…'

'Excellent. Begin at once. Make sure it's nasty and very very powerful.'

Suddenly Itoh had an idea, a marvellous idea.

'I'll make you a dragon then,' he said as he slowly folded the shape.

Saito smiled gleefully and suddenly it was there. The giant, ferocious, wicked, hideous, golden dragon laughed and roared and breathed flames. Itoh ran as fast as he could as Saito's little paper hall burned to the ground.

The dragon and Saito were never seen again. No longer did the peasants need to pay the terrible taxes. Itoh had saved them all.

Illustrated by Frances Elizabeth Livens

Nigel the Naughty Spider

by Rachel West

Nigel was a spider. Not a big spider, not a little spider, but just the right size. He lived in a cottage in the country with the Potts family.

On Monday Nigel was bored, so he decided to be naughty and scare someone.

Mrs Potts was spring-cleaning the bathroom and at that moment was cleaning the bath. Nigel very carefully dropped down a thread in front of her face. He crawled down it, hung on with his back legs, waved his front legs and grinned.

Mrs Potts screamed, ran down the stairs two-at-a-time, and sent Mr Potts up to get rid of Nigel. But Nigel crawled down the plug-hole, chuckling to himself.

Nigel didn't come out of the plug-hole until Wednesday when he decided to scare someone again.

When dinner time came, Nigel crawled up on to Master Potts's head. When Master Potts opened his mouth to put in a sausage, Nigel burped.

'Pardon, son?' said Mr Potts.

Master Potts opened his mouth and again Nigel burped. Mr Potts got very angry and sent Master Potts up to bed without any dinner. Nigel sat under the salt pot grinning.

On Thursday Nigel decided to scare Mr Potts. Mr Potts was reading his paper in his favourite armchair. Nigel crawled up the back of the chair and on to Mr Potts's head. He very carefully attached a nice strong thread to Mr Potts's glasses and slowly crawled down it. He swung backwards and forwards in front of Mr Potts's eyes.

Mr Potts tried to grab Nigel but punched himself on the nose and made it bleed. He jumped up and rushed off to the bathroom to make it better. Nigel sat on the crossword puzzle giggling.

On Friday Nigel was very tired and he was fast asleep in his web in the corner of the doorway. Mr Potts very quietly crept up underneath Nigel's web. Mrs Potts quietly crept up too. So did Master Potts. All of a sudden they all shouted, 'BOO!'

Nigel was so startled he fell right out of his web. And do you know, that bump knocked all the naughtiness out of him.

So, next time you meet a naughty spider, you'll know what to say, won't you?

Illustrated by Mick Inkpen

Time Traviler

by Gordon Semple

I am the time traviler. I am going to go on a mishen to find out what killed the Dinesores.

I need to tacke a gun and arope and climeing acwitmunt. It will be danjerus but I will do it.

I am quite clever, I will tacke a camra. Now I am redey to go.

I'm here. Now I can see a Trianasorsrex. I will take a picture of the Triranasorsrexe.

I can see a Pleseearorus and a Tradacktl. I will see lots of things.

Dinasores are vishus. They kill anamls they are bad and strong. I am in a cave I will sleep here. I will fite them of if they atack me.

This is in the morning. I am going ixsploring. I see the sun is hot. I can see the Brontosorus eating a Tadacktel. I told you they were vishus.

I think I've got the ansr. The sun is hot it macks them go to sleep. Now they are asleep. The earth is cracking. Some Dinasores will die with the sun. The earth is cracking with the sun. Lava is poring out of the cracks. The lava is kiling the Dinasores.

Now my mishen is cumpleet beecos I have found out what killed the Dinasores. Now I am going home. I am at home. I am going to get the picture dvelipt.

Illustrated by Adrienne Kennaway

The Lonely Dragon

by Joanne Haughton

Once upon a time there lived a lonely dragon. Her name was Lemon and Lime. She lived in the deep, dark, damp parts of the forest.

Why did she live there, and why did she have such a funny name? you may ask yourself. Well, she was called Lemon and Lime because she was green and yellow. Her body was green, with lots of yellow triangles down her back, all the way down to her tail.

She lived in the deep, dark, damp parts of the forest because nobody wanted to come near her. They were all too scared. When she tried to make friends with the creatures of the forest, they ran away screaming, 'There's a monster, a dirty great big monster.' Nobody liked her at all.

She was the loneliest creature in that wood. Animals threw nuts and pieces of bad fruit at her. Oh, she was so unhappy. Nobody wanted to be her friend.

One day, a vet found some badly hurt foxes in a trap, so he took them to his house and bathed their wounds. When they were better, he released them back into the wood. They had no one to look after them. Lemon and Lime thought that she would try to be their mother.

The next day she approached them and they were quite scared. 'I'm not going to hurt you. I only want to love something, and for it to love me in return.'

One fox said, 'You can't be our mother for you are a fearsome dragon.'

'No, I am not a fearsome dragon. I am a loving and kind dragon. I wouldn't dream of hurting any living thing.'

Both of the foxes wanted someone to be their mother and said that they

Adrienne Kennaway

would give the dragon a chance. The next day, the two foxes set off for school.

'Bye Mum, bye,' they both said together. They were very happy.

At school, the two foxes were telling everybody who their mother was, and what she was. Most of their mates just laughed at them and said they were telling fibs. Sally and Sam, the two foxes, were quite unhappy. They went home. They told their mum what their friends had said to them about not believing them. Lemon and Lime just smiled and said, 'Don't worry, my cubs. They don't have to believe you because you know it's true. Anyway, ask the ones who don't believe you to come round to tea and then they can see the truth.'

The next day, the two foxes went to school and picked out their mates who didn't believe them. There was Cathy Cat – 'Purr' she said. There was Terence Turtle – he just paddled about. There was Sam Squirrel – who ate nuts and ran up trees. And there was Lisa Lizard – who was a cunning little thing. Sam and Sally invited all their friends to tea on Tuesday straight after school.

On Tuesday after school, the four little creatures toddled off after school to see Lemon and Lime and to have tea. There were four little knocks on the door. Lemon and Lime opened it, and they all came in and had jelly and ice-cream.

They all lived happily ever after.

Illustrated by Alan Marks

Henry's Orange Machine

by Helen Pates

Henry was eight years old and he lived in Sweden. Henry loved to eat oranges, only oranges were very expensive in Sweden.

Henry's uncle was an inventor and he loved to invent things for Henry.

'It's not fair. I love oranges but we hardly ever buy them,' Henry complained. And so his uncle set to work on a machine that would make oranges for Henry.

While his uncle was out, Henry saw the light had been left on in the shed. So he went out to see who was in there. There was a big box covered with an old sheet. Henry lifted the sheet and peeped underneath. It was some kind of machine with lots of buttons on it. Henry couldn't help touching a few of the buttons.

After tea, Henry's uncle brought out the machine. 'Here is my wonderful orange machine,' said Henry's uncle.

'Does it really make oranges?' asked Henry.

'Just wait and see,' replied his uncle.

In the largest hole Henry's uncle put a tin of baked beans, some onion peel, six sugar cubes, some chocolate and a cupful of water. He turned it on and pressed a red button. Then he pulled a lever. After some whirring and buzzing noises, out popped a square apple.

'Stupid thing!' shouted Henry's uncle and thumped the machine. He tried to work it again as there was still some mixture left. An orange apple came rolling out this time. Henry picked it up and took a bite.

'Mmmm, delicious,' he said and gave it to his uncle to try. They were both so excited that they went outside with a box full of orange apples to sell. Nobody wanted them and so Henry and his uncle walked sadly home.

'Seeing as you liked the orange apples so much, I will let you keep the machine,' said Henry's uncle.

Henry replied, 'Thank you, Uncle.'

Henry lay in bed thinking about the machine and he reached down for an orange apple. He ate it and couldn't stop himself from eating another one. Soon, all of the orange apples in the box had gone.

The next morning Henry woke up and went downstairs for his breakfast. As soon as his mother saw him, she shouted, 'Look at you! Your skin has turned orange! Quick, back up to bed. I'll call for the doctor.'

Doctor Wills came to see Henry and said that he had probably eaten too many oranges and that he should stay in bed for a few days. When Doctor Wills had gone, Henry got out of bed and took the orange machine down from the top of the wardrobe. He took off some knobs, loosened some and tightened some, then crept downstairs to get the ingredients.

He put them in and switched the machine on. Out plopped a purple orange. Henry took a carrot and grated it into the machine. This time oranges came out. Henry was so pleased he jumped up in the air. His mother heard him thumping about and so she went up to see what he was doing. When Henry

heard her coming, he pushed the machine and the oranges under the bed and
pretended to be asleep.

When Henry was better, he brought down his orange machine and put it on
the kitchen table. He put the ingredients in and switched on the machine.
Finally an orange came rolling out, then another, then another until there
were oranges rolling off the table.

Henry's mother cut one open for him to eat, but when he smelled it, he
realised he didn't like them any more.

Henry was sick of oranges!

Illustrated by Annie Owen

Safer to be Albert

by Mark van Leuwen

One morning Albert wondered what to do.

He said, 'I know. I'll try to be an animal. I'll try to be a lion. So he got on his hands and knees.

'ROAR! ROAR!' went Albert. Tom the cat came up to Albert.

'ROAR! ROAR!' went Albert. The cat ran off, scared by Albert's lion.

Albert decided to be an elephant.

'TRUMP! TRUMP!' went Albert. He used his arm as a trunk. CRASH! He swung his arm too far and broke the vase. Mum shouted.

Albert wanted to be a monkey.

'OOO! OOO!' went Albert. He climbed the tree in the back garden.

'OOO! OOO!' he shouted from the top of the tree. Albert got stuck. He couldn't get down. His mum had to call the fire brigade to get him out of the tree.

Albert decided to be a giraffe. He went on his tiptoes. He stretched his neck.

STRETCH! STRETCH! went Albert. He didn't look where he was going. He tripped over the table leg.

Albert decided to be a snake.

'SSS! SSS!' went Albert. He slithered along the floor. He hit his head on the table. He started to cry and his mum calmed him down.

Mum gave him a biscuit. Albert decided it was safer to be Albert.

Illustrated by Toni Goffe

Hippo's Fruit Bowl

by Sophie Annesley

There was once a hippopotamus called George. He lived by a river in the country.

George had a large fruit bowl. It was his favourite thing. George sat in it whenever he sat down. It was very comfortable.

One day George got up from sitting in his fruit bowl. He went over to the river and paddled. There was something on his bottom. He looked round. It was the fruit bowl. He swished from side to side, but it would not come off.

George was very sad. He asked his friend the rhinoceros if he could pull it off. Rhinoceros was a bit grumpy and was in a rush. He didn't even hear George.

George decided to go to town to see if anyone could pull the bowl off. George went to the butcher's and asked, 'My fruit bowl is stuck on my bottom. Will you try and pull it off please?'

The butcher answered, 'I'll try, but it looks rather tight.'

The butcher tried and tried. He looked at George and said, 'I can't. I am very sorry.'

Sadly George walked out. He went into the baker's and asked, 'My fruit bowl is stuck on my bottom. Will you try and pull it off please?'

'Yes I'll try,' replied the baker. He tried and tried. 'I am very sorry, it is too tight.'

George asked everybody he knew, but nobody could pull it off.

One day George received a letter from his friend Ellie Elephant. There was going to be a big party. George wrote back saying he was very sad that he could not come. George thought it would be silly if he went to the party with a bowl on his bottom.

The day came when the party was to be held. It was snowing and the hippo was very cold. He sat in his bowl feeling very sorry for himself. Suddenly there was a loud cracking noise! It was the bowl! It had cracked. George slowly got up. The bowl had come off. It had cracked from being so cold, George thought, and he decided to go to Ellie's house.

He ran the whole way. He knocked on the door. Ellie answered, 'Hello. I thought you couldn't come.'

George just smiled. He had a marvellous time. He ate and played. Everybody enjoyed the party, but George enjoyed it most. At the end, Ellie gave 'going home' presents and guess what George got. A brand new fruit bowl!

Illustrated by Frances Elizabeth Livens

The Mouse with Big Ears

by Rebecca Bryan

There was once a little mouse who was born with bigger ears than his brothers and sisters. He always said, 'Be careful. I can hear better than you.'

All the mice just laughed at him and said, 'Just think, if a cat came along and ate up that funny old mouse.'

But Hear-all (for Hear-all was his name) did not take any notice of the other mice. For he knew that he could hear better than they could.

Just then he heard a quiet mewing noise and he said to himself, 'That must be that horrid cat, Tommy.'

He ran and told his brothers and sisters, 'RUN!' but the other mice just laughed. Hear-all ran away and the cat jumped on his brothers and sisters. And that just shows you should not laugh at others because the cat gobbled Hear-all's brothers and sisters up.

You should especially not laugh at other people who have things wrong with them, like Hear-all.

Illustrated by Rowan Barnes-Murphy

King Midas and his Touch of Jelly

by Michelle Normand

King Midas was a greedy man, but not for money – no, for jelly. He just simply loved it. He had a big fat belly, probably full of jelly. Because King Midas was so fat, Mrs Barleylove, his housekeeper, put him on a diet. He was so sad because he was only allowed jelly once every two months.

Now, one day, King Midas went out for a walk. He found a four-leaf clover and decided to make a wish. He wished that everything he touched would turn to jelly. Now, it so happened that his wish came true. To test it out, he saw a spider and he gently touched it with his hand. No sooner than he touched it, it started to quiver and wobble. It worked! He was the only king with a touch of jelly.

He ran back to the palace and asked Mrs Barleylove to give him his food early today as he was feeling a bit peckish. As soon as it came, and his housekeeper had left him, wondering why he wanted it now, he touched his food – and in a quick flash it changed into jelly.

Soon everywhere you looked was different colours and shapes of jelly. Then, what do you think? He ate it all. Even his plate and spoon turned to jelly. King Midas wasted no time in tucking into this feast, and then fell fast asleep to dream of jelly, jelly, jelly . . .

King Midas, though, after a while, got bored with this magical jelly touch and wished it would go away. Everything that he touched turned to jelly, even things like his bed. When he was walking round the palace, he tripped up and touched the floor, and all the floor around the palace turned to jelly. His servants were scared that if he touched them, they would all turn to jelly. So they all ran away whenever he came, making the king very sad and lonely.

Now, the magician who makes all the four-leaf clovers magical heard about King Midas and his touch of jelly. So, being in the neighbourhood, he decided to go and visit King Midas. As he got nearer the palace, everything he saw was made of jelly, all different colours and flavours. When he finally got to the palace, King Midas ran out to greet him, nearly shaking his hand.

King Midas told the magician all that had happened. Now, luckily for the king, the magician was a very kind man, and he said, 'If you stop eating jelly for a whole year, then the touch of jelly will be gone for good.'

King Midas had to think about this, but after a quick think, agreed. He was glad he was going to get rid of his touch of jelly, but sad because he couldn't eat jelly for a whole year.

Just before the magician left, he said, 'Everything will change back to normal. But mark my words, if you try to eat jelly before the year is up, the magic touch will come back again.'

And do you know, King Midas never, ever touched any kind of jelly again.

Illustrated by Krystyna Turska

A Tall Story

by Leigh Johnston

Once upon a time there was a clown called Candy. Candy was a member of a travelling circus. Now, as we all know, clowns by nature are very happy people whose target in life is to make people laugh.

But Candy ... well, Candy was not the happiest of people because, you see, Candy was short. Not tall, thin, fat or dumpy, but short! The result being that when he performed his funny acts, a lot of the children found it difficult to see him.

So, one day after his act, Candy went to see the ringmaster to discuss his problem. The ringmaster listened to what Candy had to say then, nodding wisely, he suggested that perhaps Candy should wear high-heeled shoes during his act.

Candy, not being the kind of person who would wear high-heeled shoes, decided to go and see Annie the Acrobat who was at that moment in the Big Top practising, and asked if he could borrow her high-heeled shoes. Annie was only too pleased to help as she knew that Candy was unhappy.

So, at his next performance, Candy wore Annie's high-heeled shoes. But, would you believe it, it didn't make any difference. The children still could not see him.

Candy was miserable and wandered around the circus with a very long face, feeling very sorry for himself. As he wandered round, he stopped to

watch the elephant keeper feeding the elephants from two big feeding buckets. Suddenly an idea crossed his mind.

Next act, there he was, striding – well, stumbling actually – into the ring with two buckets strapped to his feet.

The children clapped when Candy fell off the buckets because they were too clumsy, thinking that it was part of the act. So, even though Candy's idea had worked, it was not easy to charge around the ring with buckets tied to his feet. And so once more Candy's sad mood returned.

Candy continued to perform with the other clowns every day in an unhappy mood. Until one day, after one of the performances, a little boy called Tommy came backstage to see him. Tommy suggested that Candy wore stilts.

'Stilts?' asked Candy, puzzled.

'Yes,' said Tommy. 'They are long pieces of wood which you attach to your legs with straps, like these.'

Tommy produced a pair of long stilts which he strapped to his legs, and then started to walk about the dressing-room.

Candy's eyes opened wide in sheer delight. What joy! What wonder! They were just what Candy had been looking for.

'My dad made these for me because I wanted to be taller,' said Tommy. 'And I'm sure he wouldn't mind making a pair for you.'

So the very next day, Tommy's dad made Candy a pair of stilts which Candy practised using, until he was quite confident.

In a short while, Candy had learned to use the stilts. At the next performance, Candy walked on and everyone clapped and cheered, especially the children at the back of the audience. A special place was reserved for Tommy, who sat right at the front and clapped louder than anyone.

Candy was overjoyed to hear the children cheering, and he smiled a tall smile.

Illustrated by Nick Butterworth

Santa gets Stuck

by Rebecca Niblock and Emma Boyns

One Christmas Eve Sophie Jackson was lying in bed, thinking of the lights on the Christmas tree downstairs. Suddenly she heard a groan. It came from the chimney. She looked up quickly and saw something red fall down – a hat. It was Santa Claus! She stared, hardly able to believe her eyes. He must be stuck in the chimney, she thought. She took out her toy vacuum cleaner (which really worked) and stuck it up the chimney. Voom! Down came Santa.

'Dratted builders,' he said. 'Why don't they make wider chimneys any more?' Turning to Sophie, Santa asked, 'Do you think I could have a bath in your bathroom?'

'I think you need one,' Sophie said. 'All right, you can use our bathroom.' They went to the bathroom and Santa went in.

Sophie stood guard outside the bathroom, but then her mum came up the stairs and told her to go to bed. Sophie went back to bed, while her mum went into the bathroom. 'What a mess,' Sophie's mum said. The bath was full of water and there were black marks everywhere, but she could not see Santa because she did not believe in him. She cleared up the mess and went downstairs.

When her mum had gone, Sophie looked out of her bedroom door. Santa came out of the bathroom sparkling white. There was a funny scent in the air. Sophie asked what it was.

'Oh, I used your talc,' Santa said. As Santa seemed worried about being late, Sophie asked politely whether he wanted any help.

'Of course,' said Santa, delighted. Sophie followed him up the chimney. She had not realised that there was a ladder there (with one rung missing). Up on the roof she found Santa's reindeers and sleigh, and she patted Rudolph. Rudolph's nose glowed in the dark, lighting up the rest of the reindeers.

Off they went in the sleigh. Sophie could see the chimneys fading away in the darkness as they grew further and further away. When they stopped at the next house Santa said:

'You stay and guard the presents. I am going down.' A few minutes later he

came up again, all covered in soot. They went on like this from house to house. Finally they came to a chimney which looked different from all the others.

'I'll park the sleigh here,' said Santa. 'Hang on to me, we're going down.' Down they went, further and further, until the ashes disappeared and a white land came into sight. This, thought Sophie, must be Santa Claus's homeland – Iceland. It was snowing hard and soon they were ploughing through deep snow – up to their knees. In some parts the snow became so deep that it reached Sophie's neck and Santa had to carry her (which was quite a hard job). The snow kept falling and before long it had come up to Santa's nose. Although Santa tried to go on, he gradually found himself (and Sophie) turning into a block of ice.

Little Eskimo boys were playing in the area. When they saw a block of ice with Santa and Sophie inside they fetched a hammer and smashed the ice away.

'Phew! Close shave,' said Santa when they finally emerged.

'Almost too close,' said Sophie.

'Let's go and get the presents from my igloo now,' said Santa. It was then that Sophie woke up. It had all been a dream, she thought to herself. Suddenly she heard a groan from the chimney...